A Guide Dog is For Life
And Other Stories

Thank you for suggesting self publication. So far this has cleared almost £1000 for guide dogs and I now know how to mount the book on wheels. I thought you advice

John Hilb[ourne]

A Guide Dog Is For Life
And Other Stories

by

John Hilbourne

Disclaimer

All the Characters, except those in "Guide Dogs Are For Life " are the product of my imagination and are do not refer to anyone living or dead, except where a quotation is acknowledged.

Contents

Acknowledgements

I am highly dyslexic so I am deeply indebted to my wife Marion, for proof reading the manuscript and to Mrs June Brough for formatting it. Past and present members of the Harborne Creative Writing group, and other creative writing groups in Birmingham have made constructive comments on many of the pieces, and Guide Dogs for the Blind Association has edited "A Guide Dog is for Life" to make sure that is factually accurate when it refers to the training process and services that the association offers.

Introduction

'I thought I was applying for a guide dog; what I actually got was my life back.' So said a 35-year-old woman from Telford I met some four or five years ago. That about sums it up. That's what a guide dog has done for the 4,500 blind and partially sighted people who have one. That is what my guide dog has done for me. It is to raise money for the Guide Dogs for the Blind Association that I am publishing this book. It's not great writing. What you will find is a series of short stories, parodies, satirical pieces and limericks. It isn't even good writing but the bits and pieces it contains have amused my family, my friends and the creative writing group to which I belong. It's meant to be dipped into rather than read through at one sitting. I hope it amuses you. The profits from this will go to help other visually impaired people enjoy the same freedom to get around as you and I have

A Guide Dog is for life -Spencer the Guide Dog's Tale

(ghost written by his butler)

My name is Spencer. It's my picture on the front cover. I have been with my owner, John, for six years.

My job is to make sure that John has the same ability to get around as other people. I am very good at it. The better a guide dog is, the less his or her partner should notice what they do. John does not know half of the ways I help and protect him, and I don't want him to. It might damage his confidence and self-esteem. Just occasionally other people tell him how I have avoided a disaster and he admits he had not the faintest idea that there was a problem.

Like most guide dogs, I was born in the home of a family who agreed to look after my mother, where she was much loved. These people are called brood bitch holders. Looking after a litter of some four to ten puppies for the first six weeks of their life is not easy. Managing these puppies who are anxious to explore and chew the world and who are not toilet trained must be a nightmare at times. We stay with a brood bitch holder for six weeks, and then go to the Guide Dogs National Breeding Centre in Leamington to undergo thorough health checks.

One of the things I admire about Guide Dogs is that they care as much about us as they do about our human partners. If our partners are to rely on us, it is important that we enjoy our work and want to do it. As my owner says, "If you are prepared to walk through central Birmingham or London in the rush hour with a dog that does not want to guide you, you are very foolish". That's why, as well as the health checks at Leamington, we take part in a series of games that test whether we have both the potential and the temperament to be a guide dog. It would be unacceptable as well as unsafe for the dog, his partner or the general public if dogs who are unsuitable proceed to training. It would be cruel to train a dog who is frightened of loud noises, a dog who is very self-willed, who shies away from traffic, who cannot concentrate or is easily distracted.

I passed my tests with flying colours and for the next year I stayed with Madge and her family. Madge is what we call a puppy walker and I was her 36th puppy. During that year I learnt all the things that any well-trained dog should know, plus some of the things that a guide dog must know. It was, if you like, my primary school, and Madge and her family were my primary school teachers. They made sure I was well behaved, did not beg, pester or sit on beds or chairs. They took me to all sorts of places to get me familiar with the environments in which I would work and taught me basic skills like sitting, lying down, waiting and sitting at kerbs. I was really lucky because Madge lives in Birmingham, and that is where, as luck would have it, my partner lived.

My partner frequently says that if he had known about the way that Guide Dogs train dogs - by encouragement, reward and positive reinforcement - he would have been a much better parent. From what I have seen of human parents, most of them could learn a trick or two from my puppy walker and the people who trained me.

At the end of a year it was time for me to leave and go for advanced training. I was really sad to leave Madge and her family. We still see her occasionally and my partner keeps her up-to-date with what I have been doing.

The first three months of my training were spent at the Guide Dogs Training School in Leamington. Here we were taught all the things that any guide dog has to know. It was fun. Our trainers saw to that. We also had plenty of free time and plenty of opportunities to relax, doing what we wanted to do. The trainers took great care to ensure that any dog who was unhappy, temperamentally unsuited or lacked the abilities to be a guide dog was not asked to go on any further. I lost one or two friends, but the overwhelming majority of us made it.

For the last three months or our advanced training, we were with someone called a Guide Dog Mobility Instructor (GDMI). By this time the GDMI would have a pretty good idea of what sort of work we would be good at, and more importantly, what we would find difficult. The GDMI's job is to build on our strengths and teach us some very difficult tasks.

Despite what people believe, the responsibility to decide whether to cross the road rests with our partners, not with us. They have to listen and use their residual vision if they have any, and tell us when they think it's safe to go. However, they sometimes get it wrong. It is up to us then to stop them. It's about the only time when I will refuse to obey a command. If I decide it's unsafe I will refuse to go.

Another complex situation is when there is an obstacle on the pavement that we can't get round. We both have to work together. I will stop and sit. He will then ask me to go forward. I will then turn and sit at the kerb. He will ask me to go forward again. If I can squeeze us past I will, if not then we have to go out into the road. This is highly dangerous and we both have to work together to a set routine to ensure it's safe for us.

One of the biggest problems is parked cars blocking the pavement which means we have to go out into a busy road. I can cope, admittedly not easily, but the risks I see people having to take because someone has parked on the pavement are truly frightening.

Whilst we're in training, Guide Dogs look for a suitable partner, or 'match' as they call it. They have a large database with the characteristics of us dogs and of those who need us. Among other things, we are matched on speed, strength, temperament, preferred working environment, the type of journeys to be made, any unusual tasks we might be required to do, and so on.

Some people need a dog to take them shopping locally, to church or mosque, to the doctors and other short distances. Other people like my partner, travel all over the country, as you will see. A dog that would be happy working locally on well-known routes might not be able to cope with London Euston at 5.00pm on a Friday afternoon, air travel, strange places and routes with which they were not familiar – it would be cruel to ask them to do so. Me, I am exactly the opposite. As they say, when the going gets tough, I get going. I like it when I get to use my abilities to the full and face new challenges.

When I finished my advanced training, Guide Dogs found me what they thought would be a suitable match and took me to meet him. It was love at first sight for both of us. I was not his first dog, so he knew what he was doing and what he was looking for. As soon as he picked up the harness for a trial walk we knew we were made for each other. And so it has turned out to be.

We did the final three weeks of training together. This is easy enough to begin with, doing short circuits around quiet residential roads, but it gets progressively more difficult as we gain confidence and are introduced to tougher situations.

You learn to work together to negotiate hazardous objects, architect-designed public spaces, stations, planes and so on. At the end there is a test. It is only when Guide Dogs are satisfied that you and your partner are safe, the general public are safe and that your partner can take proper care of you that you qualify and are allowed to go out on our own. We did the three week course and qualified in eight days, not three weeks, because we were such a good match.

For the next year we were very carefully monitored. This was not only to help us with any problems we might have but to make sure that we kept up the training, were safe, and I was being properly cared for. Thereafter we get regular support visits to make sure all is well.

Let me tell you about John.

Rumour has it that he did not want a guide dog. Like many people, he thought he had too much eyesight for a guide dog and that dogs were for those who could not cope. He would find out how wrong he was!

Like most guide dog owners, he has some residual vision. He and his family tend to think that he can cope better than he can. Most of the time you would not know John has a problem because he can cope well in very familiar surroundings. It's only when things go wrong that John and his family realize how much he relies on his knowledge of where things are and on his other senses. If you left a cupboard door open, put the kettle in a different place or left a fallen branch on a pavement he has had it.

John was wise enough to apply for a guide dog after being persuaded by his friends, his GP, his ophthalmologist and Elizabeth Chapman who is a leading authority on rehabilitation.

His left eye does not work, his right eye has tunnel vision and although he can read a car number plate at a fair distance he will fall over the dustbin in front of him. He finds steps and crowds difficult. Add to this, he is slightly hard of hearing which makes crossing roads a bit dicey and he has triple vision - double vision in one eye and amblyopia in the other. He does not see in the dark or in strong sunlight. His brain has difficulty in sorting three images out so he sometimes mis-sees, sometimes gets confused and on occasions he has to close his eyes to stop having a sort of fit.

John had just retired from chairing reviews of university departments for the Quality Assurance Agency for Higher Education when I first met him – about eighty of them all told.

Without his previous two guide dogs that job would have been impossible. He was a Justice of the Peace (JP) and I used to take him to court and sit with him. I was given the honorary title of Spencer QC (Queens Canine). He was one of the cheapest magistrates on the bench. The court would have been happy to pay the mileage for his wife to drive him the two and half miles from where we live to the Victoria Law Courts in the centre of Birmingham or to pay his bus or taxi fare. John was having none of it. We walked whenever we could. As he said, 'I have never been able to walk into town before'.

He also became president of his Rotary Club and Chairman of Governors at Queen Alexandra College, a specialist further education college for young adults who are visually impaired and have other disabilities. He is a Trustee for Guide Dogs and for a short time was Vice-Chairman. This involves us travelling all over the country. Added to which, I take him to bridge, to the Debating Society, to bowls, and one or two other organisations to which he belongs. His wife says that she no longer worries when he is late coming home. She knows he is probably in the pub or has met a friend. Without me most of this would be impossible.

So you might say I have come down on all fours. I am very good at what I do, I enjoy it and everybody enjoys and admires me. I have a home where I am loved and cherished. John takes me for free runs locally, and I have a friend, Kate, who takes me out for long free runs on the Clent hills when I can be a dog like any other dog. Above all, I am not an ornament or a fashion accessory. I have a purpose and a task in the pack that is my family. I live and work with people who understand what I need as a dog, what dogs like, what adds to their quality of life and who do not treat me as a substitute child or partner.

Both my partner and I live life to the full.

A Late Date

'You are old, Mr. Williams,' the young girl said

'And your flesh is all wrinkled and tight

Yet you're after a date

And I'm telling you straight

For a man of your age it's not right!'

'In my youth,' said the old man, "I practised free love

And acquired some skill at the trade

And from many a whirl

Gained experience, girl,

 Which puts most young men in the shade'.

'You are old, Mr. Williams, 'the young girl said

 'And you've probably lost all your vigour.

To a young girl like me

Who is virile and free

Precisely what could you give her?'

 'In my youth,' said the old man, 'I went to the gym

 To build up my strength and keep supple.

Now I take two of these

And I promise to please

That's after I've swallowed a couple.'

'You are old,' Mr. Williams, 'the young girl said
'And your figure has quite run to fat.
A girl of my tastes
Prefers much trimmer waists
So what do you answer to that?'

'I have answered two questions and that is enough',
Said the old man, 'don't give yourself airs.
I've got three months to live
And a great deal to give
To a woman who shows that she cares'.

'I'm all yours, Mr. Williams', the young woman said
As she thought of a rich widow's life.
Then a voice from behind said
'I think that you'll find
He's having you on, I'm his wife.'

A Modern Fairytale

Once upon a time there was a very handsome Chief Executive. He lived in a very large house and had a very large salary. He had several share options, many holding companies, a yacht in the Mediterranean and second homes in the Caymans and the Bahamas. But he was not happy. He was, in fact, very unhappy. The richer he became, the unhappier he became.

One day his wife said to him, 'Why don't you take your secretary on a business trip?' She hoped that a change would be as good for him as the rest would be for her. So he went. But he came back even more sad.

Then his company doctor consulted his famous colleague in Vienna, Dr. Sigmund Freud. 'Can you do anything for him?' he asked.

'He should have psychoanalysis' replied Dr. Freud, 'for one hour a day every day of the year for three years.'

'But,' replied the company doctor, 'that would be very expensive for him'.

I know', said Dr. Freud, 'but I am the best there is and I do not come cheap. Besides, since he gets sadder as he gets richer, making him poorer might do the trick!'

And so it was. The Chief Executive had psychoanalysis for one hour a day each day for three years. Dr. Freud became richer and his patient a little less rich and even sadder.

Then his secretary took him to her doctor. 'You must take these tablets three times a day for six months. They are called Prozac and they work in 99% of all cases with your condition.' But they did not work for him.

One day many months later, the Chief Executive was alone in his office checking stocks and shares on his computer. As he fiddled with his mouse, there was a blinding flash of light and a little black-suited, bowler-hatted man with a briefcase appeared who was no bigger than your thumb.

Before the Chief Executive could react, that little figure said, 'I am one of the gnomes of Zürich, what can I do for you.'

'Can you make me less sad?' asked the Chief Executive.

'Nothing simpler', replied the gnome. In an instant the Chief Executive was turned into a frog. The frog lived happily, growing fatter and happier each day. Well, that is until the gnome judged him sufficiently mature to be sold for a considerable profit to a Zurich gourmet delicatessen. After all, as they say in Switzerland, gnomes will be gnomes.

Computers Have A Life Of Their Own

Life's like a computer,
Your Mac or your PC
Often unpredictable
And never error-free.

Both have books and manuals
Which tell you what to do
They may make sense to someone,
But they never will to you.

Life's like a computer.
Both call for toil and sweat
And cash and time and effort
For the few results you get.

Life's like a computer.
With age there is the risk
Both will lose their memory
And some will slip a disk

Life's like a computer.
It's inevitable they must
End up in waste disposal
And be reduced to dust.

Alice in Bankerland

Task: rewrite the first five hundred words of a classical novel to reflect a contemporary situation.

Alice was beginning to get very tired of sitting by herself at the customer help desk at the bank and having no way could she miss-sell to anybody.

Once or twice she had peeped at the screens the investment bankers were using but her colleagues looked puzzled. 'What is the use,' thought Alice, 'of having a computer if when you looked at it you could not understand what it was telling you.'

She was considering in her own mind (as well as she could, for the bank was open-plan and the chattering of her colleagues very loud) whether the return on an ISA would be worth the trouble of taking the money from her deposit account when suddenly a bowler-hatted plastic gnome, looking very flustered, rushed past her, shouting into his mobile phone, 'Buy! Buy!'

There was nothing very remarkable in that; bankers were always flustered and in a hurry. Nor did Alice think it very much out of the way to hear him then change his mind and shout, 'Sell! Sell!' Bankers were rarely consistent.

But when the gnome took a sheaf of structured investment vehicles out of his briefcase and hurried on, Alice rushed to her feet. For she had never before seen a gnome with a brief case, or indeed with structured investment vehicles. And burning with curiosity she rushed across the trading room and was just in time to see him pop through a large door into the bank's vaults.

In another moment in went Alice, never thinking how in the world she was going to get out if they locked her in.

The vault was very large and there were long rows of shelves and filing cabinets with boxes containing derivatives and files marked 'Top Secret, Bankers' Bonuses' and 'Clients' Tax Evasion Strategies'. There were documents bound up with tape marked 'Deeds of Repossessed Houses' and 'Self-certified Income Mortgages'.

Suddenly Alice came to the end of a row and tripped over a trailing electric cable which had escaped the last visit of the Health and Safety Inspectorate. She got up in an instant. There was another long passage in sight and the plastic gnome was running down it. She was just in time to hear it say, 'Oh, my derivatives, oh, my credit swaps, I'll be too late and the market will close.'

There was not a moment to lose. Away went Alice like the FT Index on a Bull Day. She was close behind the gnome when he turned another corner. She followed but he had disappeared. She walked up and down the corridor trying every door but none of them would open.

Suddenly she came across an ATM with nothing in it but a plastic credit card. Alice's thought was that it might open one of the doors in the corridor. But sadly the card slots were too large or the card was too small. Then she came across a consulting room she had not noticed before and in it a little door about 15inches high. She tried the card in the lock and it fitted. Alice opened the door and found it led into a small counting house and the largest piles of bank notes you ever saw. But sadly she was too big to get in. 'Oh, how I wish I could decrease in size, like the interest on most peoples' deposit accounts,' she said.

There seemed to be no point in hanging around so she went back to the ATM. This time she found a plastic card saying Sell Me. But wise little Alice was not going to do that, not before she had carried out due diligence. For she had read several nice little histories of people who had sold investments only to find that they could have got a better price later and had been bankrupted, or had lost their cars or houses, all because they had taken the wise counsel their financial advisers had given them.

A Pain In The Neck – His Story

Task: Write two stories about a couple, each from the perspective of one of two participants.

What was he going to do now? She was an encumbrance he could well do without. For years she had been a millstone round his neck. She had neither the social graces nor the intelligence to keep up with his career. With another woman, with Clara for example, he could have been headmaster of any school he chose. She had robbed him of that with her mediocrity and now she had robbed him of his release.

'My God', he thought as they waited for the tube to take them to Paddington. 'I deserve better than this.' Was it only four months ago he first saw the weeping red lump on her neck? She had been seated at the dressing table, putting up her hair in preparation for the end-of-term dinner party he was obliged to give. He hadn't appreciated its significance immediately; he thought it was just a rash. It was only later that evening at the end-of-term dinner party when they were talking about Matron's mastectomy and the conversation broadened out to include cancer that he began to hope. From that moment he had planned and he had schemed.

It was important for his career and his reputation that he should create the right impression. At first he thought he ought to become, publicly at least, the assiduous and caring husband. He soon abandoned that idea. Everyone in the school and in the village knew their marriage was an empty shell. But he must at least be seen as someone who had done everything possible. After her death it had to be said of him that even though it was quite obvious that the marriage had been dead for years, no husband could have done more for his wife.

The first step was to get his suspicions confirmed. He had to persuade her to see the local quack. That would not be difficult since the doctor had also been present at the dinner party. He had buttonholed the GP a couple of days later. As he expected, she had been sent for tests. The vague and evasive replies to his questions silenced his doubts. The doctor did not exactly say that she had cancer in so many words but headmasters were used to reading between the lines. He knew and he planned.

It was not appropriate that the wife of the headmaster of a private school, even a modest private school, should get treatment from the local National Health Service hospital. His status and the school image demanded the best. It must be Harley Street but not quickly for the longer he delayed the greater the chance there was that secondaries would take hold. He needed to choose his private consultant very carefully. With a few well-placed and discreet enquiries, he found what he wanted - an eminent man with an impeccable reputation and a long waiting list. Better still, when he asked the GP to arrange the appointment, he discovered that the consultant was on a lecture tour and would not be able to see his wife for at least a couple of months. The GP had implied that an early appointment with a less famous man might be wise. He had brushed this aside. 'She deserves the best and the best is worth waiting for!' he had said more than once when there were those around whom he intended to hear.

At one stage he even began to feel sorry for her. He wondered how painful it would be. It was obvious that it was beginning to hurt from the way she was moving her head. But it would not serve to alter the coldness of years. If anything, he had to intensify the gulf between them. He had read enough about cancer to know that it could be speeded up, if not caused, by anxiety, guilt and depression. He deliberately lost his temper and hurled abuse at her. He sought out her weakness, her shame in herself and her feelings of failure and he played on them with the skill of the virtuoso violinist on a Stradivarius. He saw her slowly draw more into herself and he was satisfied.

The next thing was to prepare the ground professionally. That would have to be done carefully. He thought of the members of the Headmaster's Conference. He had to find someone he could confide in but who could not keep a confidence. He thought long and hard about it. There were one or two colleagues who would fit the bill but they were not people he knew sufficiently well to talk to about a deep personal problem.

The answer, when it came, was simple. He could be far more direct. All he had to do was to get one or two of the more important Head Master's Conference members to come to his assistance. And so it was that he took the heads of three of the most prestigious private schools out for dinner in one week. He told them about his wife's illness. He told them about the Harley Street specialist and not having much hope after what the GP had said. He said that when she died he did not want to think he had to stay on at the school. He would have to get away. Had they any ideas? Each had promised to think about the matter and one had come up trumps. A charitable foundation was to fund a two-year research fellowship at one of the northern universities to do research into gifted children. It was more important that they had the right man than that he started immediately. 'Would he be interested?' His adviser continued, 'You'll still be young enough to return to headmastering. You will be away from the school while the wounds healed and at the end of the period you will have a book and several articles to your credit'. It was exactly what he wanted although he was careful to receive the suggestion circumspectly.

That had been a month ago and today they had come to Harley Street to hear the result of the consultant's tests. There was only one question he wanted answering and that was, 'How long?' Once he knew that, he could plan his new life in earnest. As they entered the consulting room the surgeon rose from his desk to greet them. The doctor took both her hands in his and looked deeply into her eyes. It was then that the blow fell. The specialist said he had conducted a very thorough examination. He had sought a second opinion to be sure that he was not making a mistake. She was suffering from a very rare skin infection which indeed would have been fatal in time, but not yet. It could now be cured. It was not cancer. All it required to clear it up completely was a course of special antibiotics. The consultant was quite excited. He said he had never seen the condition himself although he had read about it. That was why he needed a second opinion from someone with first-hand experience of the disease he had suspected. The stupid woman fainted and he had a job to prevent himself being sick.

And now the next tube was due in one minute. There would be no Fellowship, no headmastership of a well-known respected public school and no Clara. He heard the rumble of the approaching train in the distance. She moved towards the edge of the platform presumably to read the destination on its front. He knew then what he was going to do. The train roared out of the mouth of the tunnel. She leant forward, further apparently eager to find out where it was going. It would not take much to put her off balance. He put his hand on her shoulder careful to make it look as though he were trying to steady her. He began to push.

There was no resistance. For the moment, he stood there stupefied. He needn't have done anything; she was going to do it for herself.

A Pain In The Neck – Her Story

There had never been any doubt about it. She had only gone to Harley Street because he had insisted. Now he stood beside her on the platform silent and brooding. She wondered what he was thinking. What had he wanted from the day?

The indicator board showed the Paddington train due in ten minutes. As she waited she tried to make sense of it. Her mind flashed back two years. They had been on holiday in Southern France. The hotel was dirty, the disco had gone on until two in the morning and the noise of the drinkers long after that. Sleep had been impossible; its absence made the inevitable morning row even more savage than usual. In the end she left him to it.

She had found her way to the small beach, taking her path through the shattered glass of the previous evening's revelry. It was her daughter's dawn return from this that had caused the row. Not that it mattered - they would have found some other reason to fight. She spread her towel on the sand, stretched out in the warm Mediterranean sun and clasped her hands behind her neck. It was then that she felt them. They were like small pimples at the base of her neck just above her shoulder and clustering around the upper spine. There was no irritation, not even a slight itch. Even then she had known them for what they were. Of course, they could have been a heat rash, perhaps an insect bite or even the effects of the previous evening's shellfish salad. Yet she had been certain beyond any doubt and she was glad.

Her husband's sneeze brought her back to the present. She looked at him. It was like being married to a computer. In the morning she threw the switches with tea and toast and he warmed up for work. His evening cocoa closed him down for the night. There was nothing to him except his job and its exigencies. She did not exist. She did not exist as a woman, as a person, or anything else. They exchanged messages over the things that had to be done with the disguised disinterest of refined waitresses serving polite diners in a gourmet restaurant. She was his outlet for the frustration and anger he could not vent at work. Then all hell would be let loose. His eyes bulged, his teeth were bared and he hurled insult and abuse indiscriminately, not caring what he said or how he hurt her.

The pain had begun shortly after her daughter left home. Roberta had been right, there was nothing to stay for. He was a teacher. Roberta had failed educationally and therefore had failed completely. She had tried to bridge the gap between them as it widened. In the end, all she could do was to stand aside and let events take their course. Each day the pain in her heart had grown and now it was accompanied by the pain in her neck.

She had often wondered why she had married him. She had known that she was not attractive with that certainty that comes only from being told so from early childhood by a jealous and mean-spirited mother. He had seemed safe. He wore a suit. He smoked a pipe in the days when pipe smoking signified reliability rather than stupidity. He had been Head of the French department at a large private school. Surely her mother must approve! It was not that she wanted to marry him, but rather that the alternative of not being married at all seemed so much worse. And so it had happened. Marriage had seemed the lesser of two evils and she had not sought to avert it. This was a way out and she would not seek to avoid it.

It was hardly surprising that the partnership had not been successful. The first three years had been uncomfortable but her teaching had masked the underlying emptiness. Then with the birth of Roberta she had given up work. He had obtained a headmastership and they had moved. With that, she lost her friends, her colleagues and her independence. In the closed world of the boarding school, all her relationships had to be those of the headmaster's wife. She could have no friends because he had no friends. There was no one she could turn to who might have stiffened her half-hearted resolve to do something about it while she still had the chance. There was no one close enough now. No one had noticed the gradual loss of weight, the slight discolouration of her skin and the slight flinching when she moved her head. Nobody, she reflected, had cared enough. She had been safe.

He had noticed two weeks after the spots had started to weep. She was surprised it had taken him so long. She had been seated at her dressing table doing her hair prior to the end-of-term dinner. He had insisted on looking at the spots. She shuddered as she remembered his fingers probing her flesh. She had forgotten what it felt like to be touched. He suggested she might see a doctor with the same detachment that a week before he had suggested that she take her car in for servicing.

It was that bloody dinner party that ruined everything. One of the guests, the school Matron, had recently had a mastectomy. This was Matron's first time in public since the operation. Her prosthesis was not a good one and she was aware of it. Now and again she would leave the room and attempt to make an adjustment. Eventually the unequal struggle proved too much for her and she left early.

One of the guests, the school chaplain she thought it was, had remarked that it must have taken a great deal of courage for Matron to come to the dinner. After that, a discussion of cancer was inevitable. Breast cancer was a threat for many of the middle-aged women present. They sought to reassure themselves and each other by discussing its symptoms. The men simply found the topic morbidly curious. The local GP, another guest, sought to escape both his trade and his patients with no avail. He came off lightly, giving a brief description of the warning signs of early cancer like lumps and changes in warts.

Later that evening her husband had asked to examine her neck again and insisted that she should do something about it. He was clearly not surprised when, three days later, she told him that the GP had referred her to the local hospital for examination and tests. He did not for one moment care that she might have cancer. She knew full well why he had sent her to Harley Street rather than the local NHS hospital. He could say afterwards that everything that could have been done was done. Nevertheless, he took his time about arranging the appointment and that suited her.

The consultant was an elderly gentleman with silver hair who took infinite pains with his examination and apparently his appearance. He was kind, considerate and understandably noncommittal at their first meeting. He was not at all the 'Sir Lancelot' figure she had feared. The required X-rays and tests had been completed and today they had returned for the verdict. There were really only two questions to be asked: how painful would it be and how long would it take? She hoped it would be soon.

Just over an hour ago, they had been ushered into the consulting room. The surgeon rose from his desk and took both her hands in his. There was a broad smile on his face. It was not cancer. It was not fatal and it could be easily cured by a course of special antibiotics. It was, of course, a rare condition and her GP had been correct to seek an expert opinion. The specialist himself had had to seek the advice of his colleagues in order to confirm his own opinion. She fainted. She suspected that he thought it was with relief. In reality the bottom had fallen out of her world. She knew she had died as a person years ago. She had hoped that her body would soon die also. Now she would have to go on living with the emptiness inside her in the empty world her husband had created.

She heard the rumble of the tube train approaching the platform and moved towards the edge. She was frightened that he would stop her. He made no move. The train came closer. She waited until it was about 10 yards away and then fell forwards. As she did so, she felt his hand on her back giving her gentle push. 'At last', she thought, 'we are agreed about something.'

Do not put off till tomorrow what you can do to-day

The two letters came in the first post. They came in brown envelopes as official letters did in those days. Those letters changed my life. One of them very nearly ruined it! I was half dreading and half looking forward with anticipation to the post that morning, as you do when you're waiting to hear the outcome of a job interview. In the 1960s these things were handled very formally. You had to wait to be notified in writing. There was no telephone call from the chairman of the appointment panel to put you out of your misery as there is these days.

I knew the envelope with the crest of the University of London would tell me whether I had been successful or not. The second envelope took me by surprise. It was emblazoned with crest of the University of Cambridge and very much thicker.

Which to open? I have never been a very confident individual. I was even more self-doubting then than I am now. I am the sort of person who puts off knowing, preferring uncertainty to the misery of disappointment. So it was the Cambridge envelope I opened first. 'Dear Dr. Schmidt,' I read, 'Prof Rutherford has just shown me a synopsis of your recently submitted thesis for which he was eternal examiner. I should like to congratulate you on a well-conducted and innovative piece of research and a major contribution to our subject. I would like to invite you to contribute a paper to the forthcoming Max Planck conference to be held at Girton College on 15 December. I enclose the relevant information.'

I could not believe my eyes. This was the premier international conference on quantum theory in my highly specialized area and I, who had only just got my doctorate, had been asked to contribute. In some ways the offer the second letter contained of an assistant lectureship was a bit of an anticlimax.

However, I was determined to make my mark as a teacher. I had a month to prepare a course of foundation lectures introducing first-year undergraduates to their subject and to design a third-year option on quantum indeterminacy. I spent a week preparing my first lecture. It was intended to be a tour de force. As it turned out, it was an unmitigated disaster. To start with I was nervous. Then there was the lecture theatre which did not help. Foolishly I had not bothered to go and have a look at it beforehand   It was of those old tiered lecture theatres, in which the acoustic is terrible and the seats cramped and uncomfortable.. To add to my problems, someone in Timetabling had miscalculated the size of the room. A quarter of the students had to stand or sit on the floor.

I lost their attention in the first five minutes. Within ten minutes they were fidgeting in their seats, talking to each other or reading their newspapers. Worse still, the Head of Department had decided to sit in. When he came up to me at the end of the session, I was pretty sure what he was going to say and that it would not be pleasant.

'Well, my boy,' he said as he put his arm around my shoulder, 'I've come to three conclusions. Firstly, we were right to appoint you. That was a masterly presentation of the subject from which I learnt a deal and your students learnt absolutely nothing. It would have graced any postdoctoral seminar. Secondly,' he told me as he ran his hand over his balding head, 'I was mistaken in thinking that someone who had recently completed an undergraduate course would understand what first-year undergraduates needed better than more established members of the faculty' and lastly he added, 'it will do neither you nor the faculty any good if I relieve you of this course. You need to go back to the drawing board.'

And indeed I did. I had made the mistake made by many others before me of telling my audience what I knew and not what they needed to know. Throughout October I worked 120-hour weeks. At the end of the month there was another letter from Cambridge. They wanted to know what technician support I might need for my presentation. I put it on one side. I only needed a slide projector and the paper wasn't until December. It was only a 30-minute talk on my thesis, maybe tomorrow, maybe next week. There was plenty of time.

By the middle of November, I'd more or less got it right. The undergraduates were listening and their work was good. They came up to me after the lecture and asked intelligent questions. Above all, as the Head of Department noted as he peered at me through his rather thick gold-rimmed spectacles, they were enthusiastic. Indeed, students from other allied courses taught by other staff had started to come in such numbers that we had to find a bigger lecture theatre.

It was then that another letter arrived from Cambridge asking me about my accommodation requirements and enquiring whether I had any special dietary needs. I hadn't so I put it to one side. Maybe tomorrow I would get round to doing something about the paper. After all, it was only a précis of my thesis.

Then at the beginning of December I received an invitation by the conference chairman to a contributors' cocktail party. It suddenly occurred to me that I had better make a start. That night I sat down and tried to put in 5000 words and a few equations and the substance of three years' postgraduate research. After three hours I had not even written the first paragraph. Instead there was a heap of discarded typing paper, each sheet containing unsatisfactory attempts at the first few sentences. It had been a difficult week and I was tired. Maybe tomorrow when I had had a good night's sleep it would be different. Sunday evening came and went and despite sitting in front of my typewriter for another three hours nothing would come. I panicked. I spent whole days in my flat staring at a blank page. I cancelled my lectures pretending to have flu. Each day I lost confidence. I just hoped that maybe tomorrow it would be different. It never was! Eventually,14 December, the start date of the conference dawned. I knew I had the chance of a lifetime. I could rocket-launch my career. An opportunity like this would not come again. If I ducked it, I knew I would never be able to live with myself.

I had to go. I would take my thesis, a sheaf of typing paper and a portable typewriter. I would put myself in a position where I had to produce something. That night, after dinner I retired to my room and opened my machine. It was no good. At 2.00 am, I threw in the towel. In desperation I thought that if I had some sleep then may be tomorrow, if I got up early, I could do something. But there was no sleep. I was due to give my paper at 9.30 and by 9.15 I had nothing.

I knew that I could feign illness. I also knew what that would mean for me and my career. Could I start to speak and faint, or feign a seizure or something? I was impotent, like a bird mesmerised by a snake. And so it was at 9.30 I found myself in front of an audience of the world's leading particle physicists. As Sam Johnson said, 'There is nothing like an execution to concentrate the mind.' 'Ladies and gentlemen,' I said, 'I am due to give a paper on…..' It was not the paper either they or I were expecting. It was not the paper those who had read my thesis had invited me to give As I got up to speak, I realized that there was a fundamental flaw in one of the central equations on which my thesis had been based. What's more, I knew exactly what it should have been. Forty minutes later I sat down to thunderous applause. Two weeks later I received a typed copy of the tape recording of what I had said for editing. I altered not a word!

It was for that paper that I was awarded my Nobel Prize.

The Balance Of His Mind?

He was dying. He knew it. We knew it. We had all known it for some time. Liver cancer is a pretty horrible death. His GP had given him three or four months at the most and they would not be pleasant. When he invited us to celebrate his 75th birthday, we knew this would be the last time we would all get together.

There were seven of us all told, eleven if you count the young children. My wife and I had arrived from Bristol in the middle of the afternoon. We were childless but my two younger sisters, their husbands and four young children had booked into Mrs. Brown's boarding house down by the quay as we had all done this day every year for the last 15 years. The children, all of them under five, were now in bed under the watchful eye of Mrs. Tregorran. No worries there! She was a grey-haired, short and rather portly lady who must have been 70 if she was a day. She was a matronly figure and had been a great friend of my mother before the car crash which killed Mum four years ago. I still remember the scones Mrs. Tregorran used to bake for us when we were kids and her home-made strawberry jam was to die for.

The evening started with drinks and the canapés just as he liked them in the sitting room overlooking the creek. The tide was in and the sun was shining. Through the open window we could hear the subdued murmur of voices emanating from the diners sitting outside the Ship Inn enjoying the glorious sunset.

He was relaxed, with a glass of sherry taken from one of the outside caterers who he had got in to provide the meal. My younger sister, Caroline, who was a nurse looked at him sternly. 'Dad', she said, 'you know you are not allowed to drink that'. He always had a bit of a short fuse and so I waited for his reply with some trepidation. He just smiled benignly at her.

'It really is not going to make that much difference, is it?' he said. 'I have always had a glass of Tio Pepe before dinner and it's too late to alter my ways now.'

The meal was excellent. There were five courses of his favourite food accompanied by one of the best burgundies I had tasted for a long time. The Châteaubriand was out of this world and the crepe suzette just as he liked them. I personally don't like fish but even the fish pate was superb. We had all been dreading the meal. We need not have worried. We talked about the village, our journey to adulthood and the children. He encouraged us to talk about what we were doing and what we planned to do.

Caroline had, of course, one more half-hearted attempt at persuading him not to punish the burgundy. He just gave her a wicked grin and winked at the rest of us.

When the caterers retired after serving coffee, he stood up with a brandy glass in his hand.

'This,' he said, 'is the last time I shall have the opportunity of speaking to you altogether. I want to say how proud I am of you, every one of you. I have watched each of you make your way successfully in the world, dealing competently with the difficulties that life inevitably throws up. As you matured, you have changed from just being my children. You have all become my friends and unlike many families you are all friends with each other. Those of you who have married into this family have become a part of it, adding much strength and richness. Your mother, who I will shortly join, would share my pride.'

'The time has now come to say goodbye. I shall soon no longer be with you. My greatest satisfaction in life and my greatest achievement has been you. I shall pass into the next world a happy man.'

'I have just taken five of these,' he said, holding up a small medicine bottle. 'I have had them by me for some time. There is absolutely nothing you can do about it so don't even try. Let me smoke my last Romeo y Julietta and finish the remains of this excellent bottle of brandy.'

And that is what we did.

Fifteen minutes later, I took the still glowing end of his cigar from his hand.

The coroner said he had taken his life while the balance of his mind was disturbed.

Really?

A Restoration Rant

An exercise in blank verse

For now my hate has no redress
Nor has my loathing that it craves.
My anger is a futile thing,
Frustration makes me shake with rage.
Fulfillment is beyond my grasp,
My life is lost beyond reprieve.
My hope is dashed and turned to dust,
The plans I had are come to nought.
The joys that should be mine are gone
For you have taken what I want
The major target of my lust
You knew the pain that you would cause
My misery, my loss, my plight.
You knew my love of chocolate creams
To take the last one was not right!

Yet I shall have my way with you
And make you feel the pain I felt
And you'll regret the thing you've done
You'll rue the day you crossed my path

I'll make you suffer as I've done

Rejoicing in the pain you'll feel

I laid my plans, they're all complete

I've nailed my colours to the mast

Your coffee's laced with powdered glass.

Arbeit macht man Frei

Karl Marx and Adolph Hitler
Do not see eye to eye
Except that is for one thing
Das arbeit macht man frei

They differ in their politics
How they thought the world should be
But they both agreed on one thing
That it's work that makes man free.

The Pope and Martin Luther
Who were very much at odds
Both held that man was born to
Work for the glory that was God's.

They differed in their view of life
And what saves you and me.
But there's one thing they agreed about
It's work that makes man free.

And at the party conferences
In seaside towns you'll hear

From all three party leaders
The message loud and clear:

'The country's in a crisis
We're facing bankruptcy!
And it's work that's going to save us
It's work that sets us free.'

Divines and politicians claim
That work will cure all ills
But it's them that gets the freedom
And us wot pays the bills.

The Day The Earth Moved

The inquest verdict was clear. It was just and I agreed with it. Had I acted promptly and decisively, it need never have happened. As it was, I dithered and did nothing.

Of course, like most people who have been publicly shamed I have tried to excuse myself. The evidence was not entirely clear. Even the judge admitted it was ambiguous and of course it is easy to say what someone should have done after the event. But in his summing up he said 'In apportioning blame the enquiry must ask what a reasonable person would have done under these circumstances. Dr Bretherton (that's me) is an expert in this area,' he continued. 'We have heard from other experts in his field that he should have been sufficiently concerned about the unusualness of what he saw to have raised the alarm. Instead he put his own interests first. He allowed the possible damage that raising a false alarm might cause to his professional standing to override his professional judgment and his humanitarian duty. A town died that might have been saved!'

Of course I have tried to come to terms with things over the years. There are those who told me to pull myself together. It's no good crying over spilt milk, they said. What was done could not be undone, they said, and you had to move on. Believe me, I tried, I really did. But I could not escape my own feeling of remorse, of self-contempt, of self-loathing. It may be possible to meet with triumph and disaster and treat those two impostors just the same, as Kipling urges. However, I suspect you can only do that if you were not responsible for bringing them about in the first place.

Then there were those who suggested counselling. If I just let my feelings go, they claimed, if I faced myself, if I could only be honest with myself, then things would resolve themselves. But they did not. All I got by articulating what I felt about what I did or did not do was a deepened sense of worthlessness and failure.

There was a period in the psychiatric hospital with the psychotherapist. We went into my past, into my dreams, into my childhood. She certainly helped me to understand why I am what I am and why I did what I did. She pointed up the unreasonable expectations of my parents. One had won the Nobel Prize for physics and the other was a highly successful entrepreneur in petrochemicals. They were never at home, they never spent time with me and when they did they were always critical. Whatever I did it was never good enough. They made it clear they expected better things of me at school, on the playing field, the way I looked, the way I behaved, who I was. I came to realize that I had developed strategies for coping with a loveless, empty and over-demanding childhood. I know now why I became secretive and kept things to myself for fear of them being denigrated and mocked. It all made and still makes sense. No wonder I became a perfectionist, only letting people see what I had done when I knew it was fire proof. I understood why the shyness that had characterised my academic life had come about, why I found if difficult to write and give scientific papers. She suggested that the reason I ignored the evidence in front of me might in part be attributable to the damage I had suffered in childhood. But it does not wash. What is it that Shakespeare wrote, 'The fault, dear Brutus, lies not in our stars but in ourselves'.

Despite what happened, I have always kept up my interest in geology. It's been my saviour. I have not been able to practise of course. After what happened no one in his right sense would employ me. Rocks don't talk back, they don't make moral judgments, they are what they are and they do what they do with no choice. You can't blame them and they can't blame you.

That was why about a year ago I visited a university's Geology Department Open Day. We were able to visit the labs and see the latest digital equipment producing results at speeds undreamt of in my day. I was looking at one of the seismographs when I saw it for the second time in my life. Ten years ago, I had convinced myself that it was nothing, probably just a machine freak. If I had taken it seriously the peculiar earth movement that caused the damn to burst and the town to be drowned would not have occurred. The pattern I was looking at was not as strong as the one I saw then. It was indeed very, very faint, but it was definitely there.

I have just left the second disaster enquiry in which I have played a central role. The verdict was quite clear. Had the powers that be paid attention to what I was trying to tell them the Thames Barrier would still be intact. The experts tried to wriggle. They pointed out that I was discredited and non-practising. They said the pattern was very vague and unambiguous. They did not want to cause a false alarm. It had only been seen once before and so on. They could not justify closing the money markets on such flimsy evidence. The judge was having none of it.

Of course, I am sorry that all those people were drowned. But I have at last laid the ghost that has been haunting me for a decade. I can look forward to the future with some optimism.

Golden Lads And Lasses

Golden lads and lasses must
Like chimney sweeps all come to dust.

W. Shakespeare

What object would you take into a care home?

Tomorrow they will come for me. My daughter, Brenda, and her husband will pack up the few possessions I am allowed to take. I will leave this bed, this bedroom with its chintz curtains and its G-plan furniture - where Brenda was conceived, where Barbara, my wife, languished and died slowly and painfully of bowel cancer. I will totter down the stairs, into the hall over the now threadbare Axminster we were so pleased with some forty years ago. My son-in-law will steady me as I manage the three steps to the path that leads to the road. My daughter will take the house keys from me and lock the house. I shall pause and look for the last time at the rose trees and camellia bush that Barbara so cherished.

Tomorrow my world will shrink to a little room 10ft by 13 ft. It has space for a single bed, an armchair, a small coffee table and a television set, a chest of drawers and a wardrobe and that's about it. There is a communal dining hall and a large well-maintained garden over whose nurture and content I will have no input and no control. All our household goods and chattels, the product of years of careful financial husbandry, will be dissipated. My neighbours will forget me. My world will contract to the 25 other residents of Golden Years Residential Home for Senior Citizens. I shall be taking one more step, maybe the final one, on the road to the grave, on the path to oblivion.

I have spent a great deal of the time during the last two weeks thinking about which of the bits and pieces I value most I will take with me. It's not the first time I have had to make such a decision. When I was young, if I thought about dying at all it was as a physical process. Death seemed to me to come at the very end of life as the result of some terminal disease. It might be quick like a sudden heart attack, or slow and painful as with some cancers, Parkinson's or Alzheimer's disease. However it came, it would not be welcome.

How wrong I was. Most of me, the me that I am, the me I was has died already. We decline socially and mentally long before most of us decline physically. For me it began when my daughter left home. When she was at school was when I was most alive. Barbara and I were then involved in a whole host of parental work and other networks and activities. We were fully alive through our daughter, the school and our work.

When Brenda left home for university we kept her room as a sort of shrine to the past, reluctant to let her childhood go. We left it as it was long past her graduation so that she should feel at home when she came to see us. It was nonsense of course - nostalgia on a grand scale! What would a young and successful businesswoman want with adolescent wallpaper, posters of long forgotten pop stars and the now embarrassing paraphernalia of her youth?

She married and the room was no longer needed. This was the first time we went through the process I have been through in the last three months. We had to decide what to keep and what to let go. We found that no one wanted most of the things that we and she had valued. Reluctantly I took them to the tip. We were no longer as important as we once were. She did not come home now for the odd week-end. Her husband and then her children became the centre of her universe, not us. We were, or felt we were, pushed to its edge. Once again we had to contract our world,

49

deciding which bits of the relationship we wished to take into this remoter world and what must be relinquished.

Our social and psychological worlds shrank again when Barbara and I retired. The hospital where she had worked for 45 years as a nurse marked her going with a carriage clock. At first she was invited back to open days and events such as Christmas parties. Slowly she lost contact with all those colleagues she had joked and smoked with.

For me the process was sudden and more painful. I was retired early as the result of a hostile takeover. Someone had decided that all the effort I had put in, my loyalty, the skills and experience I had acquired were no longer needed. I was shown the door, thrown on the rubbish heap. Three company security men watched me clear my few personal possessions from my desk and the large array of filing cabinets that had been my fiefdom. I felt betrayed, demeaned, rejected, useless. The company was my life. It was the rock on which I had built our family security. Unlike Barbara I did not go back. There was nothing I wanted to take to remind me of my failure.

And then the process was repeated when Barbara died some four years ago. We twain were not one flesh. We were one. I managed the business and house maintenance side of our partnership. She managed the social and emotional lifeblood of our relationship. With her death that went. Again I had to decide what little of what she had I would retain to keep alive what she was – what we were. Now I must choose out of this modest collection what I should take tomorrow.

Yesterday I whittled it down to three things. Two of them, the photograph of our wedding and of us and our young family at Bognor in 1947 will cause no problem. They are not enough. I want something substantial. Something that was her, not an image of her. There is a collection of china pigs. Why she collected them I could never understand but it was well established even before we met. Then there is the medal she won for the part she played in rescuing passengers from the Harborne and Edgbaston train crash. She had gone into the debris at considerable risk to herself and five people who otherwise would not have survived owed their lives to her. But it's not her, it says a great deal about her but it's not her. My daughter can have it.

I have decided to take the Teasmade. It's old, it's battered and the teapot has brown tannin stains that my son-in-law has tried but failed to remove. For 25 years, it rested on the bedside table beside us. Each night we drank cocoa before going to bed and we would talk about our day. As she filled its kettle and put two teabags in its teapot, set the tray with two mugs, milk and sugar we would tell each other what we had done. Each weekday morning we would wake up to a piping hot cup of tea and talk about what we would do. Every weekend we would lie in bed and I would get up at 10 or thereabouts and pour the tea and then go downstairs and get breakfast. She would read the Sunday newspapers.

This was us. This was the essence of us. I will take the Teasmade with me. It will wake me up each morning for whatever time I have left. It will remind me more than anything else of what we were and what in the next world I hope we will be again.

The Knight's Tale

He was handsome and he was antique. I was sure of it! You could tell that just by looking at him. He had sharply chiselled features. There was intelligence, pride, determination and dominance. Despite the obvious distress marks that a rich and varied history inevitably leaves, he was still a fine specimen. He had such presence, such authority, such depth. I fell for him. I had to have him and the set that went with him. Only rarely do you come across chessmen of this quality and this antiquity.

I always think of chessmen as having personalities – after all, the role they play is that of surrogate warriors! Chess is a war game. The pieces are combatants representing various layers of society. As in real life, the Queen, being a woman, is the most powerful. The humble pawns, like foot soldiers, are sacrificed for the good of the major players – bishops, knights and so on. When you win a game you can imagine yourself as Alexander the Great riding in triumph through Asia Minor or Caesar crowned with oak leaves on the Lupercal in Rome. If you were French you might think of yourself as Napoleon or perhaps as Charles de Gaulle liberating France. Alternatively as a Brit you could be the Duke of Marlborough or Wellington subjugating it.

Chess is a game of skill. It's been played for centuries. It's all the battles that have ever been fought. You can replicate skirmishes which took place many centuries ago and admire the skill of the contestants. It is part of the future. Chess will be played and games fiercely contested long after our civilisation, like those it has replaced, disappears.

No wonder chess fanatics like me collect chess sets and chessmen. Top violinists need topflight violins – Stradivariuses if they can lay their hands on them. They say that these fiddles have a life and personality of their own. The musician and the instrument become a partnership, each adding something unique. The same is true of chess virtuosi and here I was in Tashkent with the opportunity to buy one of the finest antique specimens I had ever seen. It was the knight that had originally attracted me but when I picked up the other pieces they were equally fine.

I bargained with the old Uzbekistani man who was selling the set. He sat on a packing case smoking a pipe and looking as though he had not had a square meal in three days. He was in no hurry and neither was I. His long, now off-white robe was frayed at the edges with patches in several places. He had many other knick-knacks for sale, but nothing of any value.

I asked him in my halting Russian how long he had had the set. He told me he could remember his great-grandmother talking of her father playing chess with it in the court of the Great Caliph. That must have been before the Central Asian states became part of the Russian Imperial Empire in the late 19th century.

He told me he was 98 and looking at his shrivelled features I could well believe it. We bargained. He knew that what he was selling was out of the ordinary but not its real value. In the end I gave him three quarters of what he was asking. Our tour leader had told us to offer a quarter of the asking price and settle for a third. Afterwards, I felt quite mean about it and I could have paid much more for it and would have done had it been at Sothebys. Half its real value would have kept the old man and his family in luxury for years.

It proved its weight in gold. Practising with it improved my game by leaps and bounds. Next year I won the West Midlands Championship and the Bar Association's Karpov Medal and became a Grand Master. Then last night, when I was playing with a friend, the felt on the bottom of the knight came away (that is, the felt that prevents the hard base scratching the chess board) revealing some very small engraving. I took a magnifying glass to see what it was and then I read, in Russian and only with difficulty. 'Genuine antique, made in Samarkand, February 123 BC'.

It may not have been what I thought it was, but it is a very fine imitation and was the admiration of everyone who plays with it. A fake it may be but whoever had manufactured it had captured the spirit of the original on which it must have been modelled. How else do you explain the lift to my game which occurs every time I play with it?

The Best Laid Plans of Mice and Men

It was a major breakthrough. I knew it would be when I started the research. In the three years the project took to bring to fruition it became increasingly clear that the implications that my work would have for electronics and electronic engineering would be revolutionary. As you probably know, in the first decade of the 21st century it was generally believed that silicon-based electronics had reached their limit. It was thought that the number of items you could include on a silicon chip printed circuit was strictly limited and that that limit had been reached. As a result, MIT, UCL, the Planck Institute and Fermilab among others were exploring the possible uses of rare metals or neural networks. The trouble was that the chips they were pioneering would be extremely expensive to produce. I had found a way, through exploiting a little-known aspect of quantum mechanics, of increasing the circuit capacity of silicon a hundredfold. Even to me it seemed to be too good to be true. So in the last six months, as I was preparing a paper for 'Nature', I asked one of two colleagues in other universities to check my results. One of them was Professor Smith of Harvard. That is how I came to lose the patent and intellectual property rights and as well as the fame and fortune which should have properly been mine. I was determined he would not get away with it.

Revenge, as they say, is a dish best eaten cold. It does not seem likely at first when the injury is new, your heart is bleeding and you are alternatively extremely angry and very depressed. Of course I thought of publicly accusing him of theft but knew that would not work. As the real discoverers of penicillin in Oxford found, once the credit was given to Fleming, there was nothing they could do to retrieve their investment and the acclamation that truly should have been theirs. I knew right from the start that there was no point in complaining. What I needed to do with to hoist Smith on his own petard. I have thoroughly enjoyed the three years I have spent preparing the trap into which Professor Smith has fallen. Gradually the intellectual excitement associated with planning how I would get my revenge became all-consuming. I spent hours fantasising about what it would like to be Smith faced with the ignominy I promised myself I would inflict on him.

So how did I engineer Smith's downfall and regain some of the international reputation which should rightly have been mine in the first place? I am afraid I am going to have to teach you a little electronics if you are going to follow me. My early discovery stolen by that man had increased beyond anybody's wildest dreams the complexity of the circuitry that could be printed on a silicon chip. However, this could not be fully exploited because the speed at which a computer works is determined not only by the efficiency of its chip but also by the ease with which electricity can be conducted between the chip and the other components such as memory, hard drive and of course the peripherals like the printers. Think of it like a road network. Cars may be able to travel at 120 miles an hour but whether they can do so or not will depend upon whether the roads they have to travel along will allow it.

Early on I remember thinking that Smith, in hastening to steal my ideas, could not have tested them exhaustively. This was the weakness I intended to exploit. What I needed to do, therefore, was to present him with another completed project which on superficial examination and testing would work but in reality contained a basic flaw.

I had to find a way of getting the thing to him without him smelling a rat. So I put it around that I was working on a superconductor, which in fact I was, and then that I had nearly completed the project. I organised a conference at my college, invited colleagues to visit my lab and left a copy of my work where I was sure Smith would be able to find it and where, if he was careful, he could photograph the 23 pages involved without being seen.

What is it they say about the plans of mice and men? Well, I have already said I knew that Smith would not be too careful in checking in detail the work he intended to plagiarise. I never thought that Dogberry and Doolittle would be so profit-oriented as to apply the idea to the circuitry of their model T mass liner without properly testing all its component parts.

Yes, I have had my revenge. Yes, Smith went ahead as I knew he would without checking the details. He has lost his reputation, his chair and his consultancies. I was even appointed as consultant engineer to the Civil Aviation Authority's enquiry on the disaster. Not that it helps. 750 passengers lost their lives. No, revenge is not a dish best eaten cold. It is a dish best not eaten at all. As it says in the Bible, 'Vengeance is mine,' saith the Lord', it's far better left to him.

Jason

Medicine, as any doctor is wise to remember, is not a precise science. Among its disciplines forensic psychiatry is probably the most imprecise.

Being a psychiatrist of any sort is of course to sacrifice much of the income, respect, and in many instances ease of social intercourse that the status of medical doctor might otherwise confer. Many people, including those who are quite educated and should know better, think that 'shrinks' as they call us, can see into the darker aspects of their souls. Forensic psychiatrists like me are mocked by the tabloids for being soft on criminals and soft on the causes of crime. It's not true of course. As one French social anthropologist whose name I can't remember once famously said, 'To understand all is *not* to forgive all.' However, to understand much is a necessary prerequisite for helping your clients to overcome or limit the consequences of their actions.

One of the most difficult decisions we are required to make balances the freedom of the individual with the need to protect society. Let me tell you about Jason Folly.

Jason was a convicted serial killer. By the time he was eventually captured and tried he had been proved to have murdered six women in and around Birmingham. A quick glance at his file would show that the police believed that this was about half the number of women he had seriously abused. Prosecuting Counsel had no difficulty in getting a conviction. Jason confessed. So Sir John Travers for the Crown was quite happy to accept a plea of grave psychiatric illness in mitigation. Jason went to a secure unit and as far as everybody outside the prison service was concerned that was that. He should stay there for the rest of his life. For many of the tabloids even that was not enough! This is of course when he became my patient, my responsibility.

After you have been dealing with severely disturbed psychiatric patients for some time you get a nose for things and this smelt right. Jason, as he settled down to prison life, behaved exactly as the textbooks suggested he would. All the tests I applied on admission fully vindicated the diagnosis accepted by the court and repeating them made little difference to the original diagnosis and prognosis. There was no doubt about it - he was suffering from a grave psychotic illness. He believed that women who took an interest in him wanted to castrate him.

The years went by and Jason and I aged together. He took full advantage of all the medical, educational and leisure facilities the secure prison offered. He obtained a degree and then a doctorate in philosophy from the Open University. I kept his file up-to-date, recording, as we were required to do, the results of the drug therapy and tests we administered. His brain scans, when the technology became available, showed he suffered from a congenital malformation, probably because his mother had contracted German measles in the days before the MMR vaccine became widely available.

About a year ago I was sitting in my office. I was contemplating whether or not I wanted to go to a local postgraduate medical centre to hear yet another drug company sponsored lecture on the effectiveness of the latest wonder preparation for depression. I had five minutes before I needed to leave and being keen on cricket I switched on the radio to discover the score in the latest test match. England were playing Australia and doing very well. There was even the possibility that in this series they might win the Ashes. That's when I heard the news. The police had arrested a man in Brighton for committing a series of rapes and murders which were identical to some of the six that Jason had confessed to but the police had not been able to prove. A very bright young female police commander had thought it worth looking at these and comparing the DNA on record with that found in Brighton. There was a match. She then did the same for all the crimes of which Jason was convicted. Jason had not committed any of them.

The press had a field day. Yet another miscarriage of justice! PC Plod had got it wrong again. Another innocent life had been sacrificed on the altar of police performance indicators and bonuses for chief constables. None of the editorials that demanded a public enquiry into this 'scandalous affair' mentioned the fact that when Jason was convicted they had accused the police of pussyfooting around and the judge of being too lenient.

Clearly Jason was innocent. Fleet Street and Parliament demanded that the Home Secretary release him and the Home Secretary agreed. The Shadow Home Secretary, forgetting that his party was in power at the time of Folly's trial, was particularly acerbic. He asked how any court could convict on a confession backed solely by circumstantial evidence and questionable expert opinion. No one remarked on the fact, or thought it significant, that Jason still confessed his crimes and proudly boasted of them. After all, who could spend fifteen years in a secure prison without some mental damage?

For me and my profession, the question put was why had the sophisticated tools and diagnostic methods we had thrown at Jason in the year subsequent to his imprisonment not raised questions about his guilt. All I could say was that they had been correctly administered and were valid and reliable within the scientific meaning of these terms. According to these he was seriously aggressively and delusionally psychotic. In short, my professional judgment and those from whom I sought a second opinion was that he should remain sectioned and hospitalized, though perhaps in slightly more salubrious conditions.   This was the advice we offered the Home Secretary. That's the advice he made public. That's the advice for which I was pilloried in the press and eventually forced to resign. The politicians bowed to public opinion and he was set free.

I think it was Disraeli who said there were lies, damned lies and statistics. My own statistics professor used to say that in his subject there were probabilities, improbabilities but no impossibilities. The chances of any two people having the same DNA are infinitesimally small. Jason was not guilty of the crimes of which he had been convicted. On the other hand, the chances that two people with the same psychological test profile as Jason and the Brighton murderer would commit the same crimes for the same reasons are extremely high. Last week Jason Folly was rearrested. I have no need to tell you why!

Windfall

What are the feelings of those who know for certain that in 12 hours they will be dead? Dr. Johnson is reputed to have said, 'Execution wonderfully concentrates the mind.' It certainly clears it! And much to my surprise it also calms it. You are forced to face the truth about yourself! If you have been a lifelong atheist like me, there is just a chance that there is an after life and you would be wise to prepare for judgment just in case. Mostly, however, you do it because of the need to achieve harmony and closure within yourself.

I did not kill my wife. Certainly, I wanted her dead! Without doubt I had spent many fruitless hours plotting how it might be achieved. But I did not murder her! When at last the opportunity came to give her a helping hand into the hell she undoubtedly deserved, I even tried to save her!

In prison you have a lot of time to read and I have read many accounts by men and women trapped inside crippling unions. Matrimonial hatred is like nothing else. It eats at your soul, it undermines your existence. When you have lived with a control freak like my wife, it robs you of your friends, your social networks, your confidence, and your ability. That's why so many people in this situation do nothing. They have been matrimonially castrated. They no longer have the power or the will to act.

We were living in Yorkshire at the time. She decided we would go to Alton Cliffs for the day, that crumbling part of the East Coast south of Scarborough. It was early March and unseasonably warm. The sun was shining and an offshore wind was strengthening as the day wore on. There was a strong sea running. You could smell the salt from the waves as they crashed on the shore some 60 feet below.

As usual on these occasions we had had a flaming row on the way there. It culminated in the car park with each of us throwing abuse at one another and saying things that we felt but usually suppressed in order to keep the sadomasochistic union which was our marriage going. The morning had started badly. There were eight things I had done wrong or at least not done 'right' between getting up and washing up after breakfast. Some of them were deliberately provocative like not putting the top back on the toothpaste; others were genuine mistakes and oversights. Each was a mortal sin that cast into eternal damnation all those who in such marriages as ours commit them.

We had enjoyed, probably endured it would be a better way of putting it, a sandwich lunch. (One did not waste valuable money on cafes or restaurants which could otherwise be ostentatiously spent at the Women's Institute, the local church or some other charity whose members she wished to impress.) They were cucumber and tuna sandwiches as I remember them – tinned, not fresh. Just as she was pouring the second cup of tepid tea from a battered and somewhat discoloured plastic coated Thermos flask, a strong gust of wind picked up her light canvas camera case and blew it over the cliff.

She went after it despite the large warning notice about the crumbling cliff. I tried to stop her. I called her back from the edge. She would not come. She shouted that she could see the offending article stuck on a spike of a bush a few feet below the lip of the cliff and a way of getting to it. She moved nearer the edge. I called her back more urgently. She ignored me. In desperation, I leapt up and tried to pull her back. At that moment three things happened. There was a strong gust of wind which pushed us both forward. I slipped on the wet grass and the cliff edge gave way beneath her. I was left flat on the ground, hanging half over the edge with her unbuttoned cardigan flapping in my hand.

A couple sitting some 20 yards away had seen, or thought they had seen, what had happened. According to them I lunged forward and pushed. I don't think they were lying. I believe they told the court what they thought they saw.

Of course it did not happen like that and my account might have been believed but for the malicious old bitch who lived next door and exaggerated the violence of our marital discord. Then there were two other witnesses, an army officer on leave and his girlfriend. They had heard her scream at me in the car park earlier in the day. 'I know you want me dead. One day you will do it and then you'll be sorry'. I had evidently replied, 'That I will and sooner than you think.'

So there you have it. I did not murder my wife although many think I did. The wind blew her camera case over the cliff and was partially responsible for her falling with it. She claimed to be a Christian. If indeed there is a judgment day she will stand her own trial. If so I hope she receives the Justice in the next world denied to me in this.

Mother-in-law Story

As we all know, but rarely from first-hand experience let it be said, some marriages are made in heaven. So it is with mothers-in-law. Not only was my brother's marriage a case of love at first sight, it was the same with his wife's mother - instant approval on both sides. Like the relationship with his wife, this has grown into and remains something rather special. I am afraid with my mother-in-law it isn't like that at all.

Some three years ago she had a hysterectomy so we decided to take her to Portugal for a week to help her recover. It was a mistake. As Charles Dickens might have put it, we did it for the best of reasons and the worst of reasons. We knew she would need some support and we wanted to give some relief to my father-in-law, commonly referred to by his three sons-in-law as 'the victim.' As far as she was concerned, he was as a lamb to the slaughter and as the sheep before the shearer is dumb, he dared not open his mouth. We really should have known that a couple of weeks, even in a large villa, with Agatha and two teenagers was asking too much.

Agatha is about 4 feet 11 in height and at the age of 66 has the figure of a 25-year-old supermodel. She has deep chestnut hair which she would have us believe is natural. From the photographs I have seen in her youth she had clearly been a very, very attractive young lady.

Who was it who said that ageing like taxes is inevitable? She did not believe that. Now she was doing everything she possibly could to fend off increasing wrinkles and greying hair - to the great benefit of the shareholders in numerous cosmetics businesses.

When it comes to describing Agatha's personality, well, quite frankly I am lost for words. I could call her a selfish domineering bitch who would sacrifice any member of her family for the good opinion of those she sucked up to in the social circles in which she moved. But that would be insulting to canines. Virago and Harridan also suggest themselves but both imply a level of intelligence she did not possess. She was one of five sisters all tarred with the same brush. They say that blood is thicker than water. Believe me they were all pretty thick. Above all she was a control freak. Devious is not the word for it! Hypocritical too! She would use any means to achieve her own ends but God help anyone else who made the slightest deviation from the absolute integrity she required of others. The Pope only claims infallibility when he makes an ex cathedra statement. Agatha claimed infallibility in thought, word and deed wherever she was.

The holiday started badly enough. Agatha's luggage allowance was not sufficient. She would have to have some of our luggage space. Then at the airport she found she had left her purse behind and therefore had neither cash nor credit card. It was, of course, our fault. We should have reminded her! The Portuguese food was too oily and the cleaning lady (skivvy as she termed her) was not sufficiently deferential. As for the children, well, nothing they could do passed without condemnation. They were too noisy, had defective table manners, were insufficiently attentive, ungovernable, impolite, inconsiderate and so on. As to the way they dressed and the music they listened to, I leave it to your imagination.

You can imagine our relief when Agatha declared out of the blue that she was going to see the friend of the woman who would be proposing her for President of the Women's Institute on her return home and who happened to live in a village near the villa. Mother-in-law said she had promised to deliver a small package of legal papers that required signatures.

It was only a day's relief but it made all the difference. We did not even have to get her there and back. For once she returned in a benign mood. Her hostess evidently lived in a large villa and had several servants as well as the uniformed chauffeur who had driven her. Agatha had been taken on a shopping expedition and came back laden with parcels and a couple of bottles of what we were told was extremely rare vintage port. For the remaining two days of our holiday, everything was sweetness and light.

It was quite apparent that the sniffer dog at Heathrow did not think so. Neither did the two rather burly men who drew me aside - particularly when they found the brown paper package in my suit case. They reminded me that I said that I had packed the case myself and that I had said that I was not carrying anything for anybody else. Of course, I had said 'No' at Check-in. You don't think they mean members of your family, do you? What could I say? It was one of the parcels which Agatha had acquired on her shopping expedition and for which she had no room in her luggage allowance.

So I explained what had happened. I don't think for one moment she knew what she had been asked to bring into the country. If only she had had the sense to tell the truth things might have been all right. She denied having seen the parcel. That was the straw that broke the camel's back. My father-in-law, 'the victim', rebelled. He told her precisely what he thought of her. My wife and children backed him up and it was Agatha and not me who disappeared through a side door, only to reappear at the magistrates court the next day with an application for bail. She was lucky to get a two-year suspended sentence.

My father-in-law is no longer the victim of daily abuse and vilification. Remarkably, he has forgiven her and supported her through a very difficult transition. I asked him recently how he had managed to be so generous and why he had not asserted himself before. That was just before he died.

He looked surprised. 'I am a Christian', he said. 'If I am to be forgiven I must forgive others. Just as I expect to helped to be a better person so I must help them.'

It was only when the will was read that I had some idea of how much help the church had given him. How else do you explain the £150,000 he left to Mrs Simpson with whom he regularly carried the collection plate to the altar at Sunday services and with whom he retired to the vestry to count it afterwards?

My God, It Rained

That morning dawn broke like it always does in our part of the world in summer. There was purple haze over the mountains and the summit of Mount Cook glinted blood-red in the rising sun. It was unusually clear, far too clear if we had only thought about it. I stood on our verandah with Helen, my wife, enthralled and thinking how lucky we were to live where we did.

Three years previously we bought the small light aircraft, tourist and freighting firm, the house by the lake and the bed and breakfast business which went with it. My wife ran that. We and the two concerns worked well together. There was a steady flow of tourists travelling the 300 miles from Queenstown to Christchurch. Where we lived was exactly half way between the two. We had no difficulty in getting tourists who stayed overnight to take a sightseeing flight over the mountains. In summer, the view of the Southern Alps over the lake was spectacular. Few of them could resist the temptation to see them from above.

We only had four guests staying with us which was an unusually small number for that time of the year. There was a young couple, who, from the way they behaved, had only just come together, so to speak. They were trying to convince us that they were a long-established partnership. The little things gave them away. She did not know whether he took sugar in his coffee or whether he would want white or brown bread. He was far too polite and attentive! The other couple were in their late fifties and clearly bored stiff with one another. They communicated rarely and in short clipped sentences and then only if they wanted the other person to pass something or do something.

If you have never flown in a light aircraft over a mountain range, it's quite an experience. Even on calm days the turbulence can be frightening. It is not uncommon for the plane to drop fifteen or twenty feet without warning, leaving your breakfast somewhere up in the clouds. This morning was no exception. I had deliberately chosen to fly our elderly eight-seater, the smaller of the two planes we used, to add to the thrill. Perfectly safe, of course.

As we took off, the first wisps of cloud were beginning to form as we headed up towards the mountains which form the spectacular backbone of the South Island of New Zealand. Nothing unusual in that. Below, the ice-carved valleys of long gone glaciers stood out starkly in the morning sunlight rather like the prominent veins you sometimes see in the arms of the very old. Then, as we crested the range, we saw the distant coast and the two glaciers that so many tourists come to see - the mighty Franz Joseph and the slightly less dramatic Fox. From the ground, of course, glaciers can sometimes look quite dingy or speckled as the result of the dirt and rocks they have clawed away from the mountain side as they creep imperceptibly and ineluctably downward. From where we were they looked pristine white, veritable streams of piped icing sugar. That morning, they excelled themselves. They were so bright that they seemed to etch themselves into your brain. Perhaps it was the uniqueness and clarity of what we were seeing that persuaded me to do a couple of extra circuits, not that that made any difference.

It was when I turned for home that I saw it. Storms are not unusual in our part of the world. Living in a mountain area we are used to the sudden appearance of heavy dark thunder clouds and the drenching rain that accompanies them. This was something different. Suddenly the light went, all light went. Visibility dropped to nothing through the sheeting rain. The altimeter, never really reliable in this sort of country at the best of times, went wild. One moment we would be dropping what seemed like a couple of hundred feet and at a terrifying speed, only to be rocketed skywards an instant later. My passengers were terrified and so was I. All of us could hear the creaking and groaning of the fuselage. All of us watched in horror as the rain creased and rippled the fabric skin of the wings. All of us could feel the bucket seats straining at their fastenings and the seat belts cutting into us with each new upward or downward thrust of the air currents.

Under these circumstances a pilot has two choices - either to fly below the cloud and hope he can see something through the rain or try to get to the clear calm sky above the storm. In mountain country you only have one, point the nose upwards and hope you come out on top.

That's what I decided to do. We had full tanks and enough fuel for three hours. My mistake was to circle in the hope that the storm would abate as they usually did as rapidly as they developed. With hindsight, I should have headed for Christchurch or Queenstown airports where they could have talked me down. I might have made it. As it was, I climbed as high as I dared and still did not clear the cloud or the torrential rain. With every minute it became more intense. Soon the noise of it drowned out the noise of the engine and then the engine spluttered and started firing intermittently. There was nothing for it but to go down and hope we could see enough to find somewhere to land. We didn't.

I can still feel the impact. The screech of metal, the feeling of being thrown through the windscreen, seat and all, and landing in the wet grass. I remember the vivid flash of the exploding petrol tanks. Then silence. I could not move. I still can't. And the rain kept on and on.

They said I was lucky. If losing your passengers, your livelihood and subsequently your wife is lucky, if being paralysed from the neck down is luck, then they may be right.

Parental Concern – Schooling In A Market Economy

As a concerned parent, I have looked forward to the day when the latest principles of commerce and industry would be fearlessly applied in our local school. The trendy lefty who has marred the educational careers of countless generations of local children has now gone. The governors appointed a younger management-oriented product of one of the international business schools. No longer are children to be subjected to the latest educational fad of ivory tower academics who've never been in the classroom or for that matter done a serious day's work. The Headmaster is in touch with the latest thinking in organisational theory, commercial governance and management consultancy.

Immediately you enter the school you notice the difference. Gone is the old headmaster's dingy study in which piles of examination scripts were interspersed with textbooks and copies of the Times Educational Supplement. There is now a brand-new executive suite. He means business. Look at the bookshelves! You won't find a single copy of the National Union of Teachers Journal. Instead there are books such as 'The 10 Minute Teacher', 'Get by in Teaching', 'Accelerated Assessment', 'Instant Inspection', 'Rapid Rectitude' and 'Management without Tiers'. There is a large cocktail cabinet, well-stocked with a variety of alcoholic beverages which he offers to computer salesman, educational suppliers and publishers' representatives when they call. There is also a waiting area which is designed to put parents at their ease with a coin-operated coffee percolator and a receptionist with a social conscience and an evident real concern for her fellow men. She wishes everybody to have a nice day even when she has forgotten their names.

Changes in the classroom are nothing short of revolutionary. All the teaching staff have been made redundant and the funding for their positions used to create the new concept of 'learning manager'. Each learning manager leases a classroom, blackboard and chalk. Parents opt for particular subjects offered by particular learning managers. Thus, for example, a good geography learning manager will be able to cover his costs and make a living and a bad learning manager will get no students.

The Parent Teacher Association is having some difficulty in adjusting to this hard-hitting approach. The headmaster has suggested that it should appoint a leading firm of management consultants to help it with its image and marketing experts to help it with its fundraising. The rather sedate vicar who has been chairman for so long has resigned. His place is now taken by a financial consultant. As a result the Association's funds are attracting modest rates of interest from funds he manages on its behalf. They are no longer being used for short-term expenditure such as a fresh coat of paint for the school library or resources for its careers centre. You can see the sense of this. For a start, the plaster missing from many of the classroom walls can only be the result of vandalism and if replaced the damage will only recur. And again anybody worth his salt knows whether he wants to be a banker, a solicitor or accountant. Careers centres are an unnecessary luxury for those who have any spunk in them and for those who haven't they only create expectations which will never be satisfied.

The school's finances are on a much sounder basis. It is now possible to donate anonymously to the school fund. This will save generous local captains of industry with children on the waiting list the embarrassment of being publicly identified. No one using aggressive tax avoidance strategies wishes to draw attention to himself! There are, of course, a number of vicious rumours circulating that school prizes are given only to the children of parents who donate generously. There has even been the suggestion in some quarters that coursework assessments can be influenced by parental generosity. This is not true. As any sociologist will tell you, there is a clear correlation between parental income and examination results. This merely adds further evidence to support the long established observation that the greater interest wealthy families take in their children's education is reflected in their child's higher achievements.

The biggest problem so far has been with the governors. The headmaster inherited a board of amateur educationalists who had been brainwashed by the National Association of School Masters and Mistresses and the National Union of Teachers. His solution was ingenious. Each governor was offered early retirement within enhanced expenses, inflation-linked to match those he would have received had he served his full term. One cannot, of course, sell a school governorship, however tempting this may be although it would make a healthy contribution to the performance bonus the new headmaster has undoubtedly merited. Ingenious as ever, the head has opened a register of those interested in being a school governor, builder, education supplier and the like. Each new person seeking registration donates £150. They are also asked to submit a tender for their expenses and for any other goods and services they may be able to offer during the period of their tenure. The names on the register are then forwarded to head-hunters. There is thus an independent assessment of the capacity of those who put their names forward to put their money where their mouth is and conduct the school's business economically and efficiently.

Finally, the school had been declared a Community School and Academy as well as being created as a public company registered in somewhere abroad. Members of the community can buy shares in the school in return for a timeshare in the use of its playing fields, sports facilities and its computers. These, of course, have yet to be purchased.

Not content with schools in England, the head is now establishing educational interests in Northern Cyprus and Turkey. No wonder he's being encouraged by sources close to the government. They know a good thing when they see one.

School Story

It was just before Christmas. The school stood in the centre of the town bordering on the town square. It was built in the late 1880s of solid Yorkshire stone that had subsequently been blackened by the soot from the adjacent factories. They had long ceased to function. The derelict hulks of some old mills still remained on the outskirts of the town, as did the decaying winding gear of the old coalmines. Other open spaces choked with tangled weeds and the debris of demolition were apparent. It was not a pleasant place, that town. Shops were closed and broken wooden shutters now covered windows which in Christmasses past would have been filled with decorations and coloured lights. There were just one or two left, eking out a precarious living.

Last week, the old National Coal Board office which had served several mines in the region had been bulldozed to the ground. There was nothing wrong with it. It was a fine well-built structure of Portland stone which had shouted prosperity in its heyday. No environmentalist had been near the town for years. Why should they? There was no gourmet restaurant or art gallery. So a fine piece of industrial architecture from the 19th century bit the dust.

The Town Hall Clock struck 4.00 pm. The school doors opened and sixty or seventy young children spilled out and clambered over the potholes of the poorly maintained play ground, looking to see who had come to collect them. In the past, of course; it would have been mostly women - mothers, grandmothers, neighbours and so on. No longer. Now it was mostly young men, young men out of work, with fraying coats, scuffed shoes, stooped shoulders and no hope. Some of them were smoking, even though they knew it was bad for them and they really could not afford to. A few were chatting to each other but not many. There was after all not much to chat about in the third year since the last pit closed. This would be a very bleak Christmas.

The children felt none of this. For these 5-9 year-olds, the town had always been like that. Their fathers had always met them and taken them home. They were joyous. Christmas was coming. Christmas had started. They had just had their school Christmas dinner, their class party and yesterday the carol service. Each of them carried a small plastic bag tied up with red ribbon, a present from the PTA. Each of them, as they ran towards their parent, had great expectations of the coming events. Each had their dream.

There was just one solitary woman among the men. She stood a little apart, hands thrust deep in her pockets to keep them warm. She was not young, maybe thirty five or forty. It was difficult to tell in the dwindling light of late winter. Nor was the fact that she was a woman the only reason she stood out. She was much better dressed with none of the raggedness and worn appearance of the others standing there. She was looking at the school rather than the children as they bounced through the school gates.

She remained looking long after the last of the children had disappeared towards its home. Once or twice, anyone watching her would have seen her start towards the playground but each time there seemed to be something holding her back.

Thirty minutes later the lights in the building went out one by one. Then Mr Briggs, the headmaster, near retirement, accompanied by two small children, jubilant in the enjoyment of the day but exhausted by the effort it had demanded, emerged from the school door. He turned and locked it and then short-sightedly wandered towards the school exit, well satisfied.

He never saw the gun or heard the shot. The Coroner thought he would have known nothing. The young woman turned on her heel and walked away.

'That,' she said, 'is for my brother and me'.

They caught her two days later. The defence argued in mitigation that she and her brother had been sexually abused by the headmaster. It was a strong plea. Her brother had committed suicide and she had been scarred for life. Moreover, the press and the defence made much of the fact that the headmaster's continued activities would even now not have come to light had she not taken the law into her own hands. The jury was clearly impressed. The judge thought otherwise. 'Murder is murder', he said, 'and paedophilia is no excuse'. She was given a life sentence.

The Night Before OFSTED

(with apologies to Clement Clarke Moore)

T'was the night before OFSTED; all are tired and wrecked

Checking the files are complete and correct.

The staff are exhausted, and in a bad way

They've worked through the week-end for goodwill, not pay.

The Head, he's now past it, his sanity gone,

He's knocking back Prozac to try to go on.

The Management's nervous, their jobs on the line.

The teachers are furious; they've lost teaching time.

The learning resources and objectives don't match,

The classrooms are leaking, their roofs badly patched.

The stats on employment have made it quite clear

That those seeking jobs should not study here,

And truancy's rising and greater this session,

For those dodging school have got the impression

OFTED's more important and must come before

The teaching and learning they've come to school for.

And technicians and teachers are all quite aware

The review has consumed their pay rise this year.

The safeguarding policy may not be sound.

The diversity figures, they cannot be found.

Now as for promotion, it's gone by the board

And no one's been given a merit award.

Study leave has been cancelled, staff may not apply

For in-service courses to help rectify

The obvious defects that junior staff fear

That OFSTED inspectors will discover this year.

No recent updating in physics or Greek

And nothing for English where teaching is weak.

The money the school should have to use to this end

Has all been diverted and earmarked to spend

On courses some OFSTED Inspectors will sell

To school management teams who want to do well

Or to shift the blame for a dismal report

"It's the governors, teachers, and parents at fault".

But right up against it , and saddest of all

Is the haggard, distraught young vice principal

Whose job's to ensure when the inspectors inspect

They return the good grade that the governors expect;

Whose work load's tremendous with no time to think,

His marriage neglected, it's gone on the brink.

The new revised guidelines which promised so much
Have failed to deliver a much lighter touch.
He can see by the papers piled high on the floor
Obscuring the windows and blocking the door
That the only thing altered has turned out to be
The volume of paper the inspectors will see.
His head has been aching, increasing in pain.
He turns to his desk and starts reading again.
And just before daylight and just before dawn
A blood vessel's ruptured, an artery torn.

It's the night before Christmas and all round the house
No-one is sleeping, not even a mouse.
A child is heard weeping, tucked up in its bed,
"Oh, where is my Daddy? Oh, why is he dead?"
"Hush," says her Mother "there's no one to blame
He's collateral damage in the quality game. "

Sloth: A Consumer's Guide to Deadly Sins

I am not going to apologize. I have not done the work. In fact I have done absolutely nothing for the last ten days. I did not intend to. In the past I would have felt extremely guilty. I would have made all sorts of excuses but no longer. You are responsible although I don't think you intended it. Who was it who said, 'Be careful what you pray for, God might grant your wishes'. I think that the conveners of U3A writing exercises should be very chary what tasks they set. They may have results they do not anticipate. You asked me to write something on sloth. You must accept the credit for the indolent life I am now both determined to lead and to enjoy.

Shortly after the last session I got round to thinking about sin. It's not something I usually do. Being a practical man, I much prefer action to contemplation I did some research and discovered that all the major world religions believe that man, in the generic sense of course, is essentially sinful. Remember the apple in the Garden of Eden story, which is essential to fundamentalist Christianity, Judaism and Islam alike? It came from the tree of the knowledge of good and evil. Accordingly post-Eden we have a choice. In a market economy it follows that the reasonable man or woman will want to choose rationally, maximizing their returns and minimizing risk and cost. That's how I came to ask the question: which of the seven deadly sins is the best buy? Sloth wins hands down. It's the only one whose consequences you can manage to your advantage without too much risk.

Consider the other six. Gluttony compromises your health and reduces your life expectancy. Practised properly, you become so obese that you won't enjoy it anyway. Do you really want to end up with high blood pressure, heart disease and more prone to cancer, secondary diabetes, etc? Greed suffers from the same problem and the more you have, the more you want. You can never have enough. You will never be satisfied.

Then there is envy. Why envy somebody else their ox, their ass or their creative writing group? The whole point about chronic envy is that it applies to something you don't have and are unlikely to have. If you had it, you would no longer envy it. You would have to forgo the pleasure of feeling sorry for yourself or hard done by for not having it. It leads to a life of dissatisfaction, resenting what others have and you do not. If you are extremely rash you end up using unacceptable or even criminal means to obtain the object of your desire and the probability of suffering the uncomfortable consequences of doing so.

Wrath? Very unwise ! It results in all sorts of unconsidered actions with negative consequences. Read any manual on negotiation or the martial arts. They all warn you against losing your cool. If you give in to it, you lose focus, you lose judgment and ultimately self-respect. Look what happens to professional footballers, negotiators or combatants who vent their spleen   On the other hand, if you sit on it and turn it inward, it's bad for your psychological health, your physical resistance becomes lowered, your blood pressure rises, you become neurotic and suffer all the other ills the flesh is heir to.   Losing control of yourself means that you are more easily controlled and manipulated by others.

How about pride? Well, it's not ordinary pride that's meant, the sort that you might feel if you were a craftsman having done a good job or a concert pianist having given the performance of a life time.   It is overweening pride which bears no resemblance to reality. That sort of pride usually results in some sort of fall, in alienating other people and in the necessity of having to live up to a self image you cannot sustain. Other people will almost certainly try to bring you down a peg or two and in the long run they usually succeed. You are unlikely to get the adulation your high opinion of yourself warrants. Excessive pride normally comes before a fall, as they say. Politicians please note.

Finally we come to lust. Just think about it. You probably have already - several times today. Initially it seemed to me to be the most attractive. How about the freedom to do what you want with whomever it is you want to do it. A harem full of voluptuous and willing maidens perhaps? Maybe scrimmaging, so to speak, with the New Zealand rugby team, virile young men with tight backsides, prominent six packs and the stamina it takes for an hour and half of tough physical exertion. Very tempting, isn't it ? But what about the petty jealousies, the possible diseases, the heartache and all the rest of it. Seduction takes money, work and planning. Do you remember the sleepless nights of your youth lusting after the unobtainable and if you were lucky or unlucky enough to obtain it the disillusion that quickly followed? Love, as Swift points out, leads us to make the most important decisions in our lives when we are in the worst condition to do so. Lust is no different!

Properly considered, then, sloth is the rational choice. Choose any of the others and you will find that opting for one means that inevitably you will commit some or all of the rest. With sloth it is different. In this world you will not suffer any of the negative consequences and complications of choosing any of the other deadly sins – frustration, ill health, anxiety. To take one example, lust may involve coveting your neighbour's or your friend's partner, gluttony if successful because you can't get enough of them and if they are not willing, wrath because you are frustrated. Sloth is self-contained. Unlike the other deadly sins, it requires you to refrain from doing something rather than doing nothing. The damage and the evil it inflicts is limited.

There is, however, one danger. You must not lust or be greedy for Sloth. Sloth is still a mortal sin. The active pursuit of sloth to the exclusion of confession will result in your damnation. A smidgeon of self-regulation is necessary to avoid this, provided you don't overdo it.

If you go about it in the right way, you can pass it off as an illness, depression, hormone imbalance or something equally vague and difficult to diagnose or deny. You can live off the sympathy of your friends and your GP for years. I hear what you say. These are real illnesses which cause real problems for people. Of course they are and I do feel sorry for people who have them and want to get over them. I only want to be thought to suffer from them. I want the sympathy but not the angst. It's early days yet. But I've already got the Citizen's Advice people working on applying for housing benefit, disability living allowance and incapacity benefit. I have my own social worker who has organized a home help, meals on wheels and someone from the local church to do my gardening.

So I have not written anything for to-day and I have no intention of doing so in the future. I shall lie back and listen to what the rest of you have written. You won't kick me out of the creative writing group. After all, I do have a history of contributing. For all you know, I might be just deluding myself and really have ME and you wouldn't want to make it worse, would you?

The Blue Nun

This morning I made my will. I had no alternative. It was an easy matter. You see, I am fairly wealthy and have no immediate family. My wife died some time ago and although we tried everything and everybody we never succeeded in having children. It never happened.

We came closest to it on the one occasion when Barbara became pregnant. I still remember the elation we felt. All went well for the first three months. Then I was offered a partnership. Of course we celebrated. Barbara had a glass of wine - just one small glass of German Riesling. It was enough!

I think I woke up at the following morning about 3.00 am. It could not have been much later. It was midsummer and the room was still dark. I had an uneasy feeling that there was someone in the room. It disappeared the moment I saw her. There she was at the foot of our bed, a diminutive and rather squat figure surrounded by a translucent halo of light, which, although it clearly illuminated her figure, left the rest of the room in deep darkness. She was holding a kidney dish in her right hand and wearing an old fashioned Blue Nuns habit, on the breast of which was a large wooden cross.

I should have been frightened. I had always had a deep fear of the abnormal from my childhood. My uncle used to read me ghost stories, usually about malevolent spirits who were up to no good. Then there is the negative view of the other world we are encouraged to have by Hammer Films and the occasional ghost stories you hear on a Book at Bedtime.

It wasn't like that. It wasn't like that at all. I lay there completely at peace, absolutely convinced that she was a force for good. She radiated calmness, good will, love, wholesome optimism. Above all, I knew she cared! If she had chosen to speak, indeed could have spoken, I would not have been surprised to hear her repeat Julian of Norwich's joyous affirmation: 'All shall be well and all manner of things shall be well.'

My wife started to groan and thus began a long and violent miscarriage. The obstetricians found two things very difficult to credit. Firstly, Barbara had only experienced a very little discomfort; they thought she must have been in agony. Secondly, she had suffered very little internal damage. Barbara, of course, knew what I said I had seen. We both agreed that it was better not to say anything to anybody.

The second time she came, we both saw her. It was ten years ago. Barbara was in the terminal stages of spinal cancer. The hospital and the hospice had done everything they could. She could have stayed at St Anselm's but insisted on dying at home. That first night, about midnight, I woke up the way you do sometimes, knowing that something is not quite right but not knowing what it is. It usually turns out to be trivial like having left a light or the TV on or forgotten to let the cat out. Sometimes there's no reason at all. As I looked towards the end of the bed I was conscious of a growing bluishness. Slowly it became the Blue Nun-like figure I had seen all those years ago. There she was with the same habit, the same large cross on her breast and the same kidney bowl. By this time Barbara was awake. I heard a very quiet whisper from the pillow beside me. 'Thank you, Sister, I knew you would come'. And for the last three nights of Barbara's life, she did. Not only that, although Barbara felt uncomfortable, the intolerable pain she had been suffering for the past week vanished. The GP could not understand why she did not need medication. She became relaxed and more like her old self. On the third night about 4.00 in the morning, the nun made the sign of the cross and Barbara stopped breathing. Odd as it may seem to you, those last three days were some of the happiest days of our marriage.

Yes, I did ask Barbara how she knew the nun would come again. All she said was that somehow she knew she would.

Then last night I woke up to find the same figure at the end of my bed. Once again I saw the Blue Nun's habit and the large cross on her breast but this time there was a difference. There was no kidney dish. Instead she was holding one of those silver plates that some churches pass round for the collection on Sundays.

I knew what she wanted and I am more than happy to have done it. I am not now leaving all my worldly goods to my distant relatives, most of whom don't know me and don't give a damn about me. It will all go to the Order of St Brenda the Beneficent. It is the blue habit of that order that she wears.

It is now just gone ten. I feel tired, very, very tired, much more tired than usual. I am going to bed. In a very short time I expect to see my Blue Nun again. I do not expect to see the morning.

The Pavement Artist

I am a selfish motorist
I park just as I please
Are you in a wheelchair?
Well, sorry, chum, hard cheese.

I am a selfish motorist
And I don't give a damn
Obstructing mums with pushchairs
Or pushing kids in prams.

If you're forced on to the roadway
When the rush hour's at its height
And you're knocked down by a lorry
Not my fault, it serves you right.

And when I'm frail and aged
And wheelchair-bound maybe,
Feel free to block the pavement
Why should you think of me?

Too Many Cooks

Write something with as many clichés, tautologies, etc., as you can manage.

The streets of London are not paved with gold, at least not for everybody. But for Madame de Lit, they certainly had been! She was a careful woman who always looked before she leapt and knew very well how many beans make five, that a stitch in time saves nine and how many peas there were in a pod. Her business thrived because she capitalised on the fact that the course of true love never did run smooth. She knew that young men must sow their wild oats and that every dog must have its day. Her London brothel, which was established over 30 years ago, had provided her with a comfortable living, a luxury flat in Mayfair and a social network which would have been the envy of any green-eyed goddess. As she always said, 'It's not what you know, it's who you know and how you know them.'

In the early years she had rigorously looked after the pennies and the pounds had looked after themselves. Now she could afford it. She shopped till she dropped at Harrods and Fortnum & Mason's. She designer-dressed to kill and patronised the most expensive health clinics and beauty parlours. She was well aware that beauty was only skin deep, but knew that in her profession that's all it needed to be. In sum she maintained herself in the height of luxury from the depths of depravity.

She came from a long line of Italian brothel keepers. In fact you might say she had been genetically hardwired for brothel keeping. It was in her blood. For centuries her family had prospered by believing that the customer was always right. They were fully aware that you cannot buy love but you can earn a handsome profit from selling the next best thing.

Her family boasted that they had satisfied more than a dozen Popes, several European monarchs and heads of noble houses and bankers such as the Borgias and the Sforzas and even it was rumoured one contemporary Italian Prime Minister. She had been married at 16 to a 35-year-old scion of a rival firm in the hope that this would end the feud between them. It did not. She left him and the vendetta being what it is, she had to leave the country.

Running a brothel is a highly skilled business. Rome wasn't built in a day and it had taken time to build up the trust of a clientele to make the business prosper. You have to lease or buy a discreet property in an appropriate location, furnish it in a style to which your customers are accustomed. You have to have the necessary staff. There were the girls, of course but there was also the hotel side of the enterprise Someone had to manage the housekeeping side and the business finances had to be seen to. Then there is the reception desk, front of house and laundry. You needed public relations, and a good after-care to damp down any scandal and so on.

If her enterprise was to prosper, she could not afford a whiff of scandal, not with the type of clients she had. She knew that the British public believed that there was no smoke without fire. Once the press, and particularly the proprietors and editors, thought there would be more to gain from exposing her house rather than exposing themselves in it, she would be finished. She knew full well that the media believed a bird in the hand was worth two in the bush. The operation had to be smooth and free from anxiety to satisfy customers who usually felt some guilt about what they were purchasing. You had to over-staff to ensure this. Many hands make light work, as they say.

Prostitution is a demanding profession requiring that you put service before self and sometimes service before health. She never despised her customers. She just recognised that charity in the true sense of the word begins at home and if you could not get it there a little of what you fancy does you good.

Early on she realised that although her business centered on the selling of sexual services, for many of her influential clientele, sex was not what they came for. What they really wanted was protected space, protected time and, above all, the ability to talk in absolute confidence to a sympathetic ear. Many of them were workaholics with empty shell marriages. They needed a shoulder to cry on, shelter from the storm, a quiet place to recuperate. She knew that all work and no play makes Jack a very dull boy. Out there in their jungle it was the survival of the fittest. If only the public knew how many of the business, political and religious elite used her services and yet pretended to lead immaculate family lives! All that glisters is not gold, she told herself. So as well as providing the traditional offering of a brothel, she ensured that her girls were graduates and insisted that they were qualified social workers, counsellors or nurses. Her clients needed professional care, not just tea and sympathy. Given rates of pay in the public sector in these professions, she had no difficulty in recruiting.

Another thing the family tradition taught was that the way to a man's wallet/heart was through his stomach. She had recently sought to supplement her services by providing fine dining as well as fine women. And it was this that had been her downfall.

At first things went well. She knew that the labourer was worthy of his hire and even gourmet chefs, apart from TV celebrities, are not well paid. She succeeded in attracting some up-and-coming talent from some of the finest London hotels. She knew from experience that there is nothing money can't buy. Every man has his price and many enjoyed the fringe benefits that she could offer. They were capable of cooking dishes fit for a king and sometimes had to. The downside was that the hours were even more antisocial than in the restaurant and catering industry. They frequently had to produce five- course gourmet dinners at a moment's notice at three and four o'clock in the morning, particularly if there had been a long sitting in the House the night before. Soon the word got round that although the pay was good it was not worth the candle. Slowly the quality of the chefs declined.

When disaster struck it struck suddenly. It was two days before the marriage of the Duke of Randyshire. He was known to be a bit of a lad and had sown his wild oats ostentatiously and publicly. This was to be the marriage of the year. The Duke had fallen from his horse and subsequently for his nurse. She was a miner's daughter. This was not only the classic rags to riches story that had raged in the press both here and abroad for the last three months. It was also the moral tale of the depraved male transformed by the love of a good woman, a worthy successor to Florence Nightingale as The Sun put it. His official stag night was to be at the Savoy but the real event took place the night before at Madame de Lit's establishment. It was to be a night to remember. Those present included 15 peers, 22 Members of Parliament, five members of the Royal Society, 14 bankers, 12 senior members of the Confederation of British Industry and several prominent trade unionists. There were far too many for her normal staff to cope with so she had to buy in additional help from all quarters, particularly in the kitchen. Not all of guests, she knew, would take advantage of her core business offer. All of them would, however, want to eat, drink and be merry. The security people had taken over. They had turned the place upside down looking for skeletons in the cupboard. They upset her, her girls and the routine of her kitchen.

Was it Harold Macmillan who coined the phrase, 'Events, dear boy?' Three quarters of her guests went down with a particularly vicious form of salmonella the next day, including the Duke, his best man and several of his public school and hunting friends. The wedding had to be cancelled. It may be true that hell hath no fury like a woman scorned. Upset and publicly embarrass the establishment and you will really find out what true scorn is.

The official reason for postponing the wedding was kept as near the truth as possible. The public relations were suitably managed by the three Fleet Street editors and the one newspaper proprieter who had been part of the party. It was said the Duke had given a private but large dinner for his friends at a select London club. Unfortunately one of the agency chefs brought in for the evening turned out to be the carrier of a vicious strain of salmonella.

As the Prime Minister said to the Archbishop of Canterbury, 'Too many cooks spoil the brothel.'

Three Disrespectful Limericks for Christmas

Three wise men who followed a star
Went by train instead of by car.
It's rather a pity they chose intercity
To walk would have been quicker by far.

A virtuous young maid from Judea
Fell pregnant in April that year
To her man who was furious
She said, 'don't be so censorious
His Dad's the Almighty, my dear'.

A certain young queen called Victoria
Wooed a prince from north of Bavaria
In an effort to please
He imported fir trees
To add to her Christmas euphoria.